MEET POSY BATES

Helen Cresswell

Illustrated by Kate Aldous

A Lythway Book

CHIVERS PRESS
BATH

First published 1990
by
The Bodley Head Children's Books
an imprint of
the Random Century Group Ltd
This Large Print edition published by
Chivers Press
by arrangement with
The Bodley Head
and in the USA with
Macmillan Publishing Company
1991

ISBN 0 7451 1404 0

British Library Cataloguing in Publication Data

Cresswell, Helen *1936–*
  Meet Posy Bates.
  I. Title
  823.914 [J]

  ISBN 0–7451–1404–0

To Paul and Anthony with love

CONTENTS

MEET POSY BATES

POSY BATES AND THE CREEPY-CRAWLIES

Posy Bates was in her favourite hidey-hole, reading.

'Posy!' came her mother's voice from below. 'Where are you?'

Posy carried on reading. She had just got to the part where three space invaders were about to land in a playground and take over a school. It was the kind of thing she wished would happen at her school.

'Posy! Come along, I want you!'

This time Posy did raise her head, just for a moment.

'Take no notice, Punch and Judy,' she said.

Punch and Judy did not reply, for the very good reason that they were both spiders, in a jam-jar. Also in the cupboard with Posy was a stick insect called Peg the Leg, and a ladybird she had befriended earlier that day. It was quite tame, and seemed happy to wander up and down her arm.

1

'Posy!'

'Nag nag nag!' Posy told the ladybird. 'Bet your mum doesn't nag!'

She heaved a sigh and closed the book.

'Better go down, I suppose,' she told them all. 'Else she'll come up and find me. Secret, this place is.'

She climbed carefully out of the cupboard. She had made it quite comfortable in there, with cushions and a store of crisps and biscuits. She peered back at her pets.

'You'll have to stop in here, I'm afraid,' she told them. 'Mum doesn't like creepy-crawlies in the bedroom.'

She picked up the jar containing the stick insect.

'Poor old Peg the Leg! You aren't half thin. Wonder if you like crisps?'

She unscrewed the jar and dropped one in.

'I want to see that all gone when I come back!' she told it severely.

'Posy!' screeched Mrs Bates, whose name was Daff.

'Coming!'

'Didn't you hear me calling?' asked Daff as Posy entered the kitchen. She was holding the baby, Fred.

'Sorry. I was busy.'

Daff eyed her keenly.

'Those creepy-crawlies gone off your window-sill, I hope?'

'Yes, Mum,' replied Posy innocently.

'Times I've told you. Not in the bedroom. Nor anywhere else in the house, for that matter. Outdoors, that's where creepy-crawlies belong, Posy Bates.'

'Yes, Mum. But Mum...'

3

She tried again, for the millionth time.

'If you let me have a *real* pet, a dog, or even a kitten I wouldn't—'

She could tell that her mother wasn't listening. Daff thrust Fred into Posy's arms.

'Change his nappy for me, there's a good girl, while I get his feed.'

Posy gave up. She looked down at Fred, who felt distinctly damp.

'Come on, lump,' she told him, and carried him over to the sofa where she laid him down. He gazed up at her, smiling. Posy smiled back. She liked Fred, on the whole. And what was more, she was training him to be a genius. It was an experiment.

She was sure that although Fred didn't talk he could understand everything you said to him. You could tell by his expression. She was very scornful of the way Daff talked to him in silly baby language, babbling on about little piggies, and so forth.

Posy had decided to give him lessons.

'Now, where did we get to?' she asked, as she pulled off his leggings.

'Stick insects. Remember what I told you? And about spiders weaving webs that are a miracle of nature, and catching flies? Right. Now I'll tell you about . . . hedgehogs, I think. They live out of doors, and they're covered in sharp prickles.'

Fred stared up at her with eyes so round that it was clear to Posy that he was intensely interested in the subject of hedgehogs.

'They're quite tame,' she told him. 'Don't bite, or anything. And you know what? They're absolutely crawling with fleas! You *know*— I've told you about them—hop hop hop!'

Fred chortled.

'Pity I haven't got one to show you,' she said.

There was a knock on the half-open kitchen door.

'Come in!' called Daff, and in came Sam Post from next door.

'Oh. Sam. You, is it.'

'Hello, Mrs Bates. Is Posy playing?'

'No,' said Daff. 'She isn't. I've a job for her.'

'I could help her,' Sam offered.

'You could,' agreed Daff, 'and if I know anything, the job'll take twice the time to do. More hindrance than help you are, Sam Post, if your mother's to be believed.'

'What job, anyway?' Posy asked.

'I'm going to see your grandma this afternoon. I want you to go and pick me a nice bunch of flowers to take to her.'

'That's all?' Posy was relieved. She'd

been afraid that the job would take her half the morning, and waste the time when she could have been insect hunting. With any luck, she could pick flowers and spot insects at the same time.

'Easy. Come on, Sam.'

She made for the door.

'And mind you pick them with stalks long enough!' Daff called after her. 'Last ones you picked, you could hardly fit in an egg-cup, let alone a vase!'

Posy and Sam went out, past Fred's empty pram.

'My mum's a rotten name-picker,' Posy said. 'Fancy calling a baby Fred! Babies are never called Fred.'

'If people are called Fred when they're grown up, they must have been Freds when they were babies,' Sam said.

'People shouldn't be called Fred at all,' Posy said. 'It's absolutely totally a terrible name.'

Sam didn't argue. This kind of argument, he knew, could go on and on and on, and Posy always won in the end.

The Bates had a big garden, but not a particularly tidy one. It was right on the edge of the countryside, and Daff would often remark that it was hard to tell where one ended and the other began. She usually said this when Mr Bates was sitting comfortably with his newspaper.

Posy and Sam started picking flowers for Grandma. Posy liked the smells, the strong juicy smells that rose from all the green.

'Not them, stupid!' Posy told her friend. 'They're not flowers. They're dandelions.'

'Dandelions are flowers.'

'They are not. They're weeds.'

'Flowers.'

'Weeds.'

'Flowers.'

'Weeds.'

'Flowers.'

'Take them home to *your* mum, then. They're not going in my bunch.'

'My mum don't like flowers in the house. Says they make a mess and breathe up all the air.'

8

'She would,' said Posy. Then, '*Do* flowers breathe?'

'Must. Else they'd die.'

'Mmmm.' This thought had never occurred to Posy before. She peered closely at the large pink cabbage rose she had just picked.

'Wonder what they breathe *through* ...? Where's their noses?'

Sam started to giggle, despite his annoyance over the dandelions.

'You are daft, Posy Bates. Noses! Roses don't have noses!'

Posy started to laugh too, and twizzled round, chanting,

'Ring a ring o' roses
Where's the roses' noses?'

Sam joined in, and after 'Atishoo, atishoo, we all fall down!' the pair dropped breathless on to the warm grass and promptly forgot about the bouquet for Grandma.

'I'm reading an absolutely total book,' Posy told Sam. 'It's about these invaders from outer space. They're green and they've got five eyes—five! And three of 'em's just going to land in the playground of this school and take it over!'

'Wish they would at our school,' said Sam, echoing Posy's own earlier thought. 'Old Pearly'd throw a fit!'

'Foam at the mouth!'

'Lose her marbles!'

'Swallow her teeth!'

They rolled about in their mirth. Then they heard a familiar voice from nearby.

'SssssHH!' whispered Sam. 'It *is* Pearly!'

Posy followed his pointing finger and saw, moving rapidly above the high hedge, the unmistakable birds' nest hair of their teacher, Miss Perlethorpe.

'In, two three four, out, two three four, in, two three four, out, two three four!'

'Quick!' hissed Posy. 'Hide!'

'In, two three four—oh! Posy and Sam. Good morning!'

It was too late to hide. Posy, who had quite enough of Miss Perlethorpe at school from Monday to Friday, not to mention Brownies on Friday evenings, usually tried to steer well clear of her at weekends.

'Gubbins!' she said under her breath. Then, 'Good morning, Miss Perlethorpe.'

'I'm off for a jolly jog,' she informed them. 'Do you feel like a jolly jog?'

'No, thank you, Miss Perlethorpe,' the pair chorused.

'Good deep breaths! God's good air!' She took a few snorts to demonstrate.

This reminded Posy of the flowers.

'Miss Perlethorpe, do flowers breath?'

'Of course they do, dear child. All living things must breathe.'

'Then where are their noses?'

'Where are their?—' she stopped abruptly, well and truly stumped, not for the first time, by Posy Bates' incurably curious mind.

'Yes, and I've thought of something else,' said Sam. 'What about fish? Where's their noses?'

11

Here Miss Perlethorpe was on safer ground.

'Now Sam, I think you're being the teeniest bit silly. Don't you remember the tadpoles on our nature table?'

'Yes,' said Sam. 'That clumsy Vicky Wright knocked them off and the aquarium bust and they all got drownded. Dead, I mean.'

'Broke,' said Miss Perlethorpe obscurely.

They looked at her askance.

'Broke—not bust.'

'I've just thought of something else as well,' said Posy. 'Which fish have got hands?'

'You're being very silly, Posy Bates. Fishes do not have noses, and they do not have hands.'

'Where do fish fingers come from, then?' demanded Posy triumphantly.

'I've got ever so much patience,' said Miss Perlethorpe, 'but I think it's running out. Have you done your Good Deed for the day?'

'I'm doing it now.'

Miss Perlethorpe looked about, mystified.

'I'm picking flowers for my mum to take to Grandma.'

Miss Perlethorpe's gaze rested on the scattered dandelions and the single pink rose that lay nearby.

'It looks a very *small* Good Deed,' she remarked.

'Oh, we haven't finished yet,' Posy told her. 'It'll be a great big Good Deed when we have. Enormous.'

'Did you give your mother my message last night, Posy? About the Brownie camp?'

'No, Miss Perlethorpe. I forgot.'

This was not strictly true. Daff had been in such a state when she discovered Punch and Judy on the bedroom window-sill, that Posy had wisely decided to postpone asking about the Brownie camp.

'Well remember, do!' Miss Perlethorpe was off again on her jolly jog. Her voice floated back to them. 'And remember—Brownies lend a hand!'

'Silly bat!' said Sam. 'Glad I'm not in the Brownies.'

'You'd look sweet in the uniform,'

Posy told him. 'Little brown frock and nice white ankle-socks.'

But Sam was not listening.

'Hey. Look—what was that?'

'What? Where?'

'There!' He pointed.

Posy turned just in time to see a shaking of the leaves in the shrubbery.

'Oooh—was it a cat?' To Posy, a cat would be second best to a dog.

'Don't think so.'

Cautiously they approached. Nothing moved. Very carefully Posy parted the foliage. She gasped.

'Oh! Oh Sam, it's a hedgehog!'

It was. Curled under a flowering redcurrant and now fast asleep, it seemed. It was crystal clear to Posy Bates that it had plonked itself there so that Fred could see his very first hedgehog.

'Oh brilling, oh total!' crooned Posy Bates. 'What day is it? Saturday the tenth of May—my lucky day!'

Sam stared dubiously at the hedgehog.

'Wonder how it washes itself?' he said. 'Can't can it? Must go all its life

14

till it drops dead without washing behind its ears. Lucky thing!'

'Have hedgehogs *got* ears?' Posy was going from roses with noses and fish with fingers to hedgehogs without ears.

'Don't seem to hear us,' Sam agreed. 'Should've thought it would've scooted. They can scoot like mad, hedgehogs.'

Posy was thinking fast.

'They're full of *fleas*!' she exclaimed joyfully. 'They're full of creepy-crawlies!'

She could kill two birds with one stone. Fred could have a good look at a hedgehog *and* fleas!

'I'm having this,' she announced. 'As a pet.'

'Pet? What—take it walkies on a lead? Where'll you put the collar? Where's its neck?'

'It's a walking insect collection. And I need it, to show Fred. Now—how are we going to get it up to my room?'

'I'm not picking it up,' said Sam promptly.

'You stop there and watch it,' Posy told him. 'If it tries to run, chuck your anorak over it.'

15

She ran back towards the house and the shed. There she scanned swiftly about, then seized a shovel and an empty sack.

'You're never putting it in there!' exclaimed Sam, shocked. 'It'd get all its needles stuck. It'd be cruelty to hedgehogs.'

'Course not. Watch!'

Posy knelt down. Using the sack in much the same way as Daff used folded tea-towels to lift hot dishes, she gently lifted the hedgehog and placed it on the shovel.

'Not dead, is it?' The hedgehog showed little sign of interest.

'Now,' said Posy, 'this is what we'll do. Mum's in the kitchen feeding Fred. I'll wait by the back door, and you go round the front and ring the bell. Then, while Mum's answering, I'll nip in the back and up the stairs.'

'What'll I say when she opens the door?'

'You won't say anything,' explained Posy patiently. 'Because you won't be there. You'll ring the bell, then beat it. Scarper.'

'OK,' said Sam.

They left the bunch of flowers for Grandma lying forgotten in the hot sun. Cautiously they approached the house.

'Go on, hurry!' said Posy. 'If I stand too long like this, it might drop off.'

'And break all its bones,' said Sam. 'Have hedgehogs got—?'

'Hurry!' hissed Posy.

He fled.

Posy waited. She looked fondly down at the earless, neckless, boneless hedgehog that was nevertheless swarming with fleas. She was dying to get it up to her room to have a good look at it under the magnifying glass. She peered through the window by the door and could see her mother with Fred on her knee.

'Where's he got to? Why doesn't he get on and ring that bell?'

Posy had forgotten that the front door bell did not work. She waited.

'Ooooh!' Exasperated, she looked about her for a convenient hiding place. 'Oh—only for a minute. Won't do any harm.'

She placed the hedgehog, still on its

shovel, carefully in Fred's pram, then ran round the house. Sam was peering from behind a laurel bush by the front door.

'What're you waiting for? Do it!'

'I have! I've done it three times!'

'Well, bang on the door, then. Do it fast!'

She fled. She was half-way round the house when she heard the scream. Daff, about to lower Fred into his pram, had found a squatter.

'Oh, *buggins*!' Posy had meant to say 'gubbins', but it came out wrong.

She was tempted to run for it. But Posy Bates, once she had her mind set on something, did not give up easily. She rounded the corner, whisked the shovel from the pram, screaming, 'Sorry, Mum! It was only for a minute!' and ran back round the house. At the front door she pushed Sam unceremoniously aside.

'Quick!' she gasped.

She was through the door, up the stairs and then safe in her own room. She shovelled the hedgehog under the bed.

'Don't move!' she ordered.

She ran back out, closed the door behind her in case the hedgehog disobeyed (or did not hear, having no ears), and let out a deep breath. Posy Bates had her walking collection of creepy-crawlies and Fred Bates would soon have his very first glimpse of a real live hedgehog. Explanations would come later ...

POSY BATES AND THE
BAG LADY

One of the best things about having an elder sister, thought Posy Bates, was that she got picked on, too. Pippa, who was fifteen and went to the big school in Nottingham, got picked on a lot.

Another good thing was that she and Pippa could get together and grumble, and sympathize with one another. Not that Pippa had had much sympathy the time Daff discovered the hedgehog in Posy's bedroom. In fact, she had screamed nearly as loudly as Daff herself.

It had been there for a couple of days, hobnobbing with Punch and Judy and Peg the Leg. Posy took it into the garden for secret airings, and called it Holly.

Whenever she saw the chance, she took Fred out of his pram and upstairs to continue his education.

'D'you see what I mean about the prickles?' she asked him. 'They're called spines. Remember that.'

Fred did not look as if he were remembering much, or even looking properly at the hedgehog. He seemed more interested in one of Posy's slippers, which he put to his mouth and sucked.

This was what he was doing when Daff came in. She took one look at Holly and the slipper, and screamed. She snatched up Fred who dropped the slipper and bawled. She went running off to dunk him in the bath and drown all the fleas. Fred, who had already

been bathed only an hour earlier, bawled the more.

Posy slunk downstairs with Holly in a box and put it in the shed.

'And you're not just putting it back in the garden either, Posy,' Daff told her. 'I know you. It'd be back inside in no time.'

So Posy's father, George, had driven off with Holly in the box in the back of his van. He was decorating a house with a big garden in the next village.

'It'll be right as rain there,' he told Posy. 'Shouldn't be surprised if there isn't a whole nest of them there already.'

'Hedgehogs don't have nests,' said Posy. She kept hoping that perhaps they had homing instincts, like pigeons. For days afterwards she had combed the garden, and put out secret saucers of milk for when Holly returned, alive with fleas.

This particular Saturday morning Daff was edgy and Fred was cutting a tooth and Posy was definitely being picked on. She was halfheartedly polishing the brass candlesticks when

Pippa came down.

Daff was rattling pots in the sink.

'Oh, you're up, are you?' she said. 'Near ten o'clock, Pippa Bates.'

This, from Posy's point of view, was a good start.

'I wish you'd call me Philippa,' said Pippa. 'It is my name. And you gave it me. Though I can't think why,' she added.

This was even better.

'When you've got kids of your own, then you can pick their names,' returned Daff. 'I picked yours, and that's that. I called you Philippa because I liked the name Pippa.'

'But I'm fifteen now!' wailed Pippa. 'I feel daft, with a name like that. *Can't* you call me Philippa?'

'No,' said Daff. 'I can't. Too much of a mouthful, for a start.'

'No more than yours,' argued Pippa. 'Not much more—one extra syllable, that's all.' She counted them with her fingers on the table. 'Daph-ne. Phil-ipp-a. There!'

'Yes,' said Daff. 'And when have you ever heard anyone call me Daphne?'

23

Pippa was floored. Everyone called her mother Daff, from Grandma to the milkman.

'Now, get your breakfast and then get the table cleared,' Daff went on. 'It won't do, up this time every Saturday.'

'I'm a growing girl,' said Pippa. 'Growing girls need their sleep. Miss Gisborne says so.'

'It's not Miss Gisborne who gets held up with breakfast when it's near dinner time,' said Daff.

'Miss Gisborne's lovely,' said Pippa dreamily. 'Dead trendy. You should see her hair. Her first name's Tracey. Wish mine was.'

'And I suppose you're straight off on the bus to town, the minute you've finished chucking cornflakes all over the place,' said Daff.

'Course. What's there to do round here?'

'Plenty,' Daff told her. 'I find plenty.'

'Where's the shops, where's the discos, where's the—'

'We've a perfectly good shop,' Daff told her. 'Stocks near everything, that

24

Post Office does.'

'Oh yes! Like trendy gear and the top twenty and—ooh Mum, while I think—*can* I have my ears pierced?'

'No,' said Daff. 'You cannot.'

'Here we go!' thought Posy. 'The Big Ear-Piercing Row!'

It had been going on for as long as she could remember.

'But you said I could when I was fifteen. You said—'

'You're fifteen for another year yet. The minute you get your ears pierced, you'll be fancying yourself grown up. Twenty-five I was, before I had my ears—'

'We know. You told us. But that was in the olden days, Mum.'

'Oh, thanks very much!'

'All the girls have them done now. And the boys.'

'*And* their noses,' said Daff. 'I've seen them. Horrible.'

The baby began to cry outside.

'Drat!' she said. 'There goes Fred!'

'You're a really rotten name-picker, Mum,' Pippa told her. 'Fancy calling a baby Fred. Babies are never called

25

Fred, they're called things like—'

But Daff had already gone.

'She is a rotten name-picker,' Posy said. 'Wish I was called Samantha. Or Rebecca. Or Vanessa.'

'Yours is better than mine,' said Pippa. 'Pippa! Sounds like a hamster or something!'

Posy giggled.

'Can I go to town with you?' she asked.

'No, you can't. You're a menace, trailing round after me.'

Posy had a particular reason for wanting to go to Nottingham. Daff came back in.

'That's him off,' she said, meaning Fred.

'Mum, can I go into town with Pippa? Got to get your birthday present.'

'You could get something up at the shop,' said Pippa.

'Can't. You said so yourself. Want a tin of baked beans for your birthday, Mum? Or a packet of soap powder? Very total. Or . . .'

Posy got her way in the end.

'Now, mind you catch that half-past-twelve bus back,' Daff told them. 'And you don't let your sister out of your sight, Pippa, do you hear me?'

'I'm not a baby,' Posy said, once they were on the bus. 'You don't have to keep an eye on me.'

'And I'm not a baby-sitter,' said Pippa.

'It's not as if you have to cross roads, or anything,' said Posy. 'And you couldn't be kidnapped, not in the

Victoria Centre.'

'That's true. Shouldn't think anyone'd want to kidnap you, anyhow.'

Posy did not argue.

'And another thing,' said Pippa, 'once you start wandering about you'll go into a dream and clean forget about Mum's birthday present and end up without one.'

'No I will not,' said Posy.

'I bet you will. I know you.'

'It's what I've *come* for. Couldn't forget, could I?'

In the end Pippa agreed that they should split up, and meet by the clock at twenty past twelve.

'And mind you're there,' she warned. 'If we miss that bus, Mum'll have our guts for garters.'

Posy Bates had two things to buy. Her mother's present, and something she had set her heart on ever since reading the book about moths and butterflies. She was going to buy a buddleia. This, according to the book, was a large shrub that, if unpruned, would grow as high as a tree. It had long purply spikes and attracted

28

butterflies. They flew to it like wasps round a jam-pot.

'I'll have millions of butterflies,' she thought. 'And they'll be my pets, and I'll have names for them all. And Mum can't complain, because you don't have to take butterflies for walks, *and* they don't keep having kittens.'

Daff was very firm on the No Pets rule. It was her long-running row with Posy, like the one with Pippa about pierced ears.

The Victoria Centre had two gleaming floors of shops and an indoor market. It was like Aladdin's cave, with its magical Emmett clock that you could stand and watch all day, if you had time. Today Posy didn't have time. She set off at a brisk trot. She scanned to left and right of the arcade, looking for a tree shop. She was not much tempted to dawdle, because most of the windows were full of boring things like clothes and shoes. Butterflies, she felt sure, were not interested in these.

She did allow herself a sortie into W. H. Smith, where there was a book she was reading. Whenever she came to town she went and read another chapter, while Daff did her shopping. She had already read several books this way.

'Oh, gubbins, it's gone!' said Posy Bates indignantly. Such a thing had never happened before. 'They've gone and sold my book!'

The shelves were filled with plenty of others, of course, but today she didn't have time to choose another. She stomped out, cheated of her chapter.

By the time she was half-way along the upper floor of the Centre, Posy was beginning to feel that this was not her lucky day.

'Rotten shops,' she thought. 'Where are all the trees?'

That was when she saw the bag lady. She was sitting on a bench all by herself. This, Posy guessed, was because nobody wanted to sit next to her. She was the most downright mucky and ramshackle person Posy had ever seen. Her grizzly nest of hair poked out under a woolly hat and her grimy fingers with their black nails poked out from fingerless mitts. Her shabby bags bulged. Posy was enchanted.

'Hello!' she said.

She knew, of course, that she should not speak to strangers, but felt that the bag lady did not count.

'Hello,' she said again. 'I'm Posy Bates.'

The bag lady considered her with pale, watery eyes.

'I dare say,' she replied at length.

'Are you stopping here long?' asked

Posy conversationally. 'Have you come a long way?'

She knew from television programmes that bag ladies spent their days trudging the streets, and at night slept in cardboard boxes under bridges.

'Far enough. Where's your ma?'

'Back home,' Posy told her. 'As a matter of fact I've come to choose her a birthday present.'

As soon as the words were out she could have bitten her tongue. Some sure instinct told her that bag ladies didn't get birthday presents—perhaps didn't even remember when their birthdays were.

'I bet you have a really interesting life,' she said hastily. 'Going about and seeing everything. I bet it's really interesting.'

'I dare say *you* get proper cooked meals,' said the bag lady sourly. 'I dare say your belly don't rumble a deal.'

'Oh it does!' Posy assured her. 'As a matter of fact, it's rumbling now. Well ... almost rumbling.'

She thought delightedly how shocked her mother would have been to hear the word belly instead of tummy.

'As a matter of fact, my belly often rumbles,' she said daringly. 'My belly's often empty.'

'Poor you, then,' said the bag lady. 'And poor me. Snap!'

She had a deep, croaky voice. That was probably on account of sleeping under bridges, Posy thought, even in the winter. She gazed consideringly at the old lady. At first she had thought she was fat, but now saw that she was merely bundled up in layer upon layer of grimy clothing. She had a sudden inspiration.

'You wait here,' she said. 'I'll be back in a tick. Don't go away.'

She ran off back the way she had come, and into a shop whose enticing smells she had sniffed as she passed, and which really had made her tummy rumble—or almost rumble.

'I'll have a carrier, please,' she said, when her turn came. 'And I'll have a small pork pie, and two of those and three of those—ooh, and one of those, and . . .'

All in all she spent nearly three

pounds, but by now had clean forgotten the buddleia, let alone the birthday present. She had done exactly what Pippa said she would do—except that she was certainly not in a dream.

The bag lady was still sitting there, squat and immovable among the milling shoppers. Posy let out a sigh of relief. Already she thought of her as a friend.

'Here I am! Wait till you see what I've got!'

She plonked herself on the bench with her own bag on her knee.

'Something to stop our bellies rumbling,' she confided. 'Well, yours mostly. I'll just have an egg sandwich with cress, I think.'

The bag lady squinted sideways. Posy proffered the carrier. Out came a mitted hand. It delved into the bag and came up with the pork pie. Then the pie was being crammed into her mouth and the bag lady was munching and swallowing, munching and swallowing, and crumbs stuck to her chin and her teeth rattled, clickety clack.

'You can't expect her to have

manners,' thought Posy, and she ate her own egg sandwich as rudely and noisily as she could, for company. It tasted a thousand times better than any sandwich eaten in a normal, polite way.

'*That's* stopped my belly rumbling!' she said, with her mouth full of the last huge bite. Shreds of egg flew from her lips. But the bag lady, having devoured the pork pie, was now tearing at a portion of cold barbecued chicken. Posy watched, fascinated.

'She certainly hasn't got any table manners,' she thought. 'But come to that, there isn't a table.'

She wondered whether to invite the bag lady back home for dinner. She imagined her sitting at the kitchen table, with her pompon cap and tattered mitts. Wisely, she decided against this.

'There's plenty left,' she said encouragingly. 'Enough for your tea as well.'

Her companion looked set to polish off the contents of the bag at a sitting.

'Don't want to give yourself belly-ache,' she went on.

35

Champ champ champ. There would clearly be little conversation at this picnic. Suddenly, out of the blue, Posy remembered where she was and where she was meant to be.

'Gubbins!' She looked at her watch. 'Help! Got to go! Oh, sorry, but I've got to. Here!'

She thrust the bag of food into the old lady's arms.

'Wait!' spluttered the bag lady, mouth full. She stooped and delved into one of her own bags and took something out and pushed it into Posy's hand. 'Here!'

Posy looked down. It was a wooden reel, an empty cotton reel.

'Bobbin!' said the bag lady obscurely. 'Lucky bobbin! You take it!'

'Oh, thank you!' It was not an empty cotton reel at all, it was a bobbin, a magic bobbin, given by a real live bag lady who was herself more than a little magic.

'Goodbye!'

She put the bobbin into her pocket and ran, ran for the clock and Pippa and the twelve-thirty bus. She ran from

36

magic back to reality.

She decided to say nothing about her strange meeting, not to Pippa, not to anyone.

'What did you get Mum?' asked Pippa as the bus drew off.

'Oh, gubbins!'

'Well, what did you get?' asked Pippa. Then she saw Posy's face. 'Oh, no! Don't tell me! You forgot!'

Posy did not reply. She had done worse than forget. She had spent the money on beautiful food for a hungry old lady. She had some money left, but not enough for a birthday present *and* a buddleia. Either the buddleia or the present had to go. Money, unlike butterflies, didn't grow on trees.

Posy gazed miserably out of the window and heard Pippa scolding on and on. She put her hand in her pocket and felt the magic bobbin.

'If you're really magic,' she told it silently, '*do* something!'

She actually closed her eyes. And then, smooth and silent as only magic can be, the idea slid into her head.

'Wait and see,' she told Pippa mysteriously.

And that afternoon she persuaded her father to take her to the Garden Centre in the next village. There she bought a strong green buddleia in a pot. She tied a bow on it and hid it in her cupboard, and next day gave it to a delighted Daff.

'Happy Birthday!' she said. 'And Happy Butterflies!'

Posy Bates was having her cake and eating it. And what was more, she had a magic bobbin from a bag lady.

POSY BATES AND THE BIG SUNDAY AFTERNOON BANG

For Posy Bates, each day of the week had a different colour—a different flavour, even. She could tell a Monday from a Thursday, or a Wednesday from a Saturday with a kind a sixth sense. The day of the week she could pick out from all the others even with her eyes shut, was Sunday.

Sundays, she had always known, were grey, grey and tasteless (apart from the roast beef and Yorkshire pudding that was like an oasis in a seemingly endless desert). Posy's parents believed that Sunday should be a day of rest.

'That's really old-fashioned,' Pippa was always telling them. 'Trust you to think that, when everyone else is going to Adventure Parks and the seaside!'

'Saturdays are for that,' said George, who wasn't firm about most things, but was about this.

He liked, as he often said, 'to know

what's what'. He liked to wash his hair
on Fridays and the van on Saturdays.
He liked the alarm clock to ring at
7 o'clock exactly and always fetched
fish and chips for supper on Tuesdays.
Above all, he liked Sunday to be
Sunday—a day of rest.

'Saturdays and school holidays,' Daff
agreed.

This particular Sunday was going to
be even more boring than most. Pippa
had gone to stay with a friend, and
Amy, Posy's four-year-old cousin, was
being dumped on the Bates' family for
the day.

'You can look after her, Posy,' Daff
told her. 'Nice to have someone to play
with.'

'Play with?' Posy was disgusted.
'She's a baby!'

'You can take her to Sunday School
with you in the morning,' Daff said.
'Miss Price won't mind.'

So they went off together, and Amy
drew pictures of lopsided angels and
sheep, and Posy quite enjoyed herself,
too. She happened to like stories, and
the ones in the Bible were as good as

40

any others. She could tell them to Fred,
later. If he was going to be a genius, he
should definitely know some Bible
stories.

'Come round to my house after
dinner,' Posy told Sam on the way
home. 'We'll think of something to do.'

By the time dinner was over Posy was
ready, as usual, for anything. Sunday
afternoons were truly awful. It was
almost as if something actually
happened to make time stop—if
anything, it seemed to go backwards.
On Sunday afternoons her parents went
to sleep. They did not call it sleeping,

they called it 'having five minutes'. Daff actually went up and lay on the bed, once Fred was settled. George, after a look at the paper, sank back in the armchair and shut his eyes. Usually he snored.

This particular Sunday was in June, and it was sunny. That meant they were allowed in the garden as long as they did not play ball games, and kept their voices down to whispers. (This was because the Posts next door had five minutes, too.)

Amy was playing with her building bricks. The air was still. Posy glared at the quiet garden.

'What Sunday afternoons need is a big bang,' she thought.

And no sooner had she thought it than she realized that this was one of her inspirations. Sam came into sight and she waved furiously.

'Listen,' she told him, 'what we're going to do is make an explosion!'

He stared.

'We're going to do an experiment to make the most ginormous bang that'll wake everyone up for miles. We'll mix

42

things nobody's ever mixed before, and we don't know *what*'ll happen. I just hope it'll go off with a bang.'

'I want to mix,' said Amy instantly. Mixing was one of her favourite things to do.

'What kind of things are we going to mix?' Sam asked.

'Anything!' Posy was afire now. 'We'll wait till Mum and Dad are asleep, then go back in. If we stand on a kitchen chair we can get to all those packets and bottles in the cupboard. There's lots of stuff up there—real stuff, from the chemist's.'

'Where will we mix it?' Sam asked. 'What if we blow the house up?'

'I know,' said Posy. 'We'll dig a hole, here in the garden, and put a big basin in it, and then mix in that.'

'What *sort* of things?'

'Oh—mustard, salt, vinegar, washing-up liquid, milk—everything!'

Posy shivered deliciously at the dangerousness of it. A girl at school had told her only last week that it was dangerous to eat oranges and milk together. She said they curdled up in

43

your stomach and made poison. This sounded very likely to Posy, and she had stopped taking oranges to school.

What, then, might happen if you mixed marmalade and milk together? Posy Bates decided to take the risk. There was really no choice. By now the special Sunday afternoon quiet had descended like a blight over the whole neighbourhood. Even the birds were subdued, as if they had been warned of the consequences of loud whistling on a Sunday afternoon.

'Come on!' she urged.

'Let's mix!' agreed Amy happily, and trailed after them.

They tiptoed into the house. It was depressingly quiet. They could hear only the buzzing of a fly and the sound of George's snoring from the next room.

Posy edged a chair across the tiles, and, standing on it, began to hand down bottles, packets and tins. Sam took them and put them on the table. Soon the shelves were nearly empty. Posy climbed down and looked at the collection, awestruck.

44

Sam picked up a packet.

'Boracic,' he read. Then another, 'Bicarbonate of soda. *Should* we, do you think?'

'Not here! I told you—in the garden. Wait, and I'll go and fetch some of those little plastic building-cup things of Fred's. We'll tip a bit of everything into each.'

Once the actual work began, Posy enjoyed it. She measured liquids and powders into the multi-coloured cups. She used a mustard spoon, because it seemed safer. She noticed that Sam was using a soup spoon, shovelling out the ingredients with an abandon that was a little alarming.

'Me, me!' squeaked Amy.

To keep her quiet they gave her a plastic bottle of washing-up liquid and let her squirt it into a jam-jar. She seemed to enjoy this very much, and it could not possibly, Posy thought, be dangerous.

They put all the cups on to a tin tray and carried it out into the garden.

'Now,' said Sam, 'where shall we have the hole?'

'Not too near the house,' said Posy instantly. She wanted a bang, all right, but she also wanted her home to be left standing.

'Not too near,' Sam agreed. 'Here, look, by the hedge.'

He took a trowel and began to dig a hole between the hollyhocks and the hedge.

'We'd better have it deep,' he said. 'You keep watch, and make sure no one's looking.'

Posy stared about her. The gardens were quiet. She looked up at her mother's curtained window, then at the Posts'. There was no sign of life anywhere. All the world, it seemed, was having 'five minutes'. Amy was making a hole of her own, using a spoon.

'Right!' said Sam at last. Carefully he fitted an orange plastic mixing-bowl into the hole. 'Come on—let's mix!'

He picked up two of the little cups, hesitated, then threw the contents in. Posy could feel her heart thudding. She picked up two cups and did the same.

'We've got to keep stirring it,' she

46

said, and used a garden cane to do it. 'Get things all properly mixed in.'

They went on tipping and stirring, tipping and stirring, till all the powders had gone.

'Nothing's happened!' Posy was not sure whether she was glad or sorry.

'Don't worry,' said Sam. 'It will.'

It seemed to Posy that he was getting bossy about things. It was, after all, her idea and her explosion.

'That's only the dry stuff,' he said. 'Wait till we put the liquids in. *That*'ll do it!'

He took a yellowish liquid—cough mixture? He stood well back from the

hole and threw it in. They waited, then bent cautiously over and looked.

'It looks horrible,' said Posy. 'Ugh—and can you smell it?'

A thought struck her.

'Could it turn into poison gas, d'you think?'

'Could,' he said. 'Better try not to breathe too much.'

Posy took her stick and bravely started to stir again as one by one the liquids went in. She tried to hold her breath, but in the end gave up for fear of bursting.

The mixture now certainly did smell—and look—disgusting. It looked the kind of mixture that might easily up and explode at any moment. Posy poured in the last cup of vinegar, and jumped back.

'Come on!' she commanded. 'Bang!'

Nothing happened.

'Don't look as if it will,' said Sam dubiously. 'Pity.'

They stood and gazed down into the orange bowl. Had it not been a Sunday afternoon, Posy might have left it at that. But it was, and tea-time was still light-years away. The gardens lay deserted under the hot sun.

'Come on!' she said. 'There's heaps more stuff in the house. I'll make a bang or bust!'

They went into the pantry and took some of nearly everything, from currants to tomato ketchup. Posy even broke an egg into the hole. It floated on the brown mixture like an evil yellow eye.

After that she became giggly, because it seemed to her that what they were making now was a kind of omelette—and omelettes do not, as a rule, blow up.

Sam, on the other hand, went quiet. He was absolutely determined now to get that explosion.

'It won't half be a bang!' he muttered now and then. '*Won't* there be a bang!'

Amy trotted back and forth, happy as a sandboy. Neither Posy nor Sam dreamed of keeping an eye on her. After all, the hole was not deep enough for her to drown in.

'I've got an idea,' said Sam at last. 'I'm just going back to my house to get something.'

When he came back, he had a tin.

'Stand by,' he ordered. 'This'll do it!'

Posy hoped so. She watched as he spooned a great heap of the white powder into the murky liquid.

'Oooooeeeeh!'

Posy's scream was so long and loud that it frightened even herself, and she clapped her hands over her ears to shut it out. Then she ran towards the house and safety, still screaming and still seeing that awful foaming, seething mass, suddenly alive and dangerous.

'Idiot!' yelled Sam after her. 'It was only fizzy liver-salts!'

'Look!' It was Amy, in the pantry. Posy looked. She screamed again. Amy was covered in blood.

It was not blood at all, as it turned out. It was tomato ketchup. It was all over the pantry floor as well, and so were a couple of packets of tea, a whole bag of flour, and a lot of sugar and gravy salt. Here and there floated the evil yellow eyes of eggs.

'Oh, gubbins!' said Posy Bates, and had never meant it more.

'I mixed,' said Amy happily.

Then Daff was there too, and George, dazed and bad-tempered from being jerked out of their five minutes. Both, in fact, livid.

'What? What the—?'

Posy and Sam exchanged glances. There *was* going to be an explosion that Sunday, after all . . .

POSY BATES—INVENTOR

Posy Bates was sitting up in her room thinking. She did quite a lot of this, for an eight-year-old. Not that anyone else believed it—especially grown-ups.

'I just wish you'd stop and think, Posy,' Daff was always saying.

'Do you ever *think* what you're doing?' Miss Perlethorpe would sigh.

This particular day Posy Bates was thinking about thinking. This had been triggered off by watching a man on television showing how to make things out of empty yoghurt cartons. He had made desk-tidies, spill-holders, key-rings, mobiles—he had gone on and on. By the time he was finished, Posy thought it very likely that the whole world could be made out of empty yoghurt pots.

This had set her thinking. In the past she herself had made all kinds of things from cornflake packets, yoghurt pots, matchboxes and jam-jars. On Daff's dressing-table there still stood a decorated jar for cotton wool balls that Posy had made once for Mothering Sunday. But so far, everything she had made had come from an idea of Miss Perlethorpe's, or a television programme.

Now, Posy was so enchanted by the infinite possibilities of yoghurt pots that she had decided to change the world.

'You don't *have* to put coal in a coal-bucket,' she thought. 'You could plant a tree in it, or take it shopping, instead of a basket. And you don't *have* to use blankets on your bed. You could cut them up into small squares and use them as kettle holders.'

There seemed no limit to what you could do if you really thought about it. And Posy Bates meant to think about

it. She intended, in short, to become an inventor.

'I reckon being an inventor's the next best thing to being a witch,' she told Peg the Leg. 'Absolutely total.'

He, being a stick insect, did not respond. He was the fifth Peg the Leg she had had so far this year. Posy yearned for a pet, but Daff put her foot down, and said no. So Posy was reduced to a procession of spiders, snails, ladybirds, stick insects, hedgehogs—anything that moved, really. (The only things she had drawn the line at so far were worms. Even Posy Bates could not see *them* as pets.)

But she knew very well that it is not kind to keep such things in jam-jars and boxes. So she kept them only a few days, then set them free. Then she found some more, and kept them instead. And as one spider looks very like another (except perhaps to its own mother) and one stick insect like the next, she always gave them the same names. Then she could pretend they *were* the same—real pets.

'Better get started straight away,

54

then,' she remarked to Punch and Judy. They showed as much interest as you would expect a pair of spiders to show.

'Now, what first?'

'Posy!'

It was Daff calling, and already half-way up the stairs, by the sound of it.

'Oh, bumboils!'

Posy scrambled out of the cupboard and shut the door. She managed to be sitting innocently on her bed, reading, when Daff poked her head round the door.

'Oh, there you are! Nose in a book, as usual.'

Privately, Posy thought that in a book was the best place for any nose to be, but wisely said nothing.

'I want you to fetch me some things from the shop. Come along, now, look sharp!'

She was gone. Posy followed her, wondering how to look sharp. She didn't see how anyone could actually *look* sharp, even if they were.

'Here's the list.'

Posy took it, and the money, and went out.

'A bag!' Daff called after her. 'You'll want a bag!'

'Oh no I won't!' thought Posy. She fished the metal coal-bucket out of the shed. Then she scooted off, before Daff could call again.

She enjoyed the novel feeling of swinging a coal-bucket instead of a bag or basket. It creaked and rattled and was more company, somehow. It also made the boring business of being sent up to the shop seem actually rather exciting, fun even.

'It's not a bucket or a bag or a basket, it's a baskle, busket, bagget, bugget...'

'Hey wait, Posy!'

It was Sam Post running after her.

'Where are you going?'

'Shop.'

'What've you got *that* for, then?' he asked, pointing at the bucket.

'Put things in,' Posy told him airily.

'*Put* things in? What, the shopping, you mean?'

'Course.'

56

'But what *for*? You don't get coal, not at the shop.'

'I'm not getting coal. I'm getting gravy powder, a dozen eggs, half a pound of bacon and a pound of sausages.'

'And you're putting them in *there*?'

'I told you.' Posy stopped. 'Look—what's the difference between a coal-bucket and a basket?'

He stared.

'There isn't one. They've both got handles and they both hold things. There!' Posy was triumphant.

'But . . . you use baskets for shopping and coal-buckets for coal.'

'You might,' Posy told him loftily. 'I don't.'

She was tempted to add 'Because I'm an inventor', but decided not to. If Sam couldn't catch on to the coal-bucket idea, he wasn't going to catch on to the other things she had in mind. Or that she *vaguely* had in mind. She rather wished Sam would go away and leave her in peace, to think up her inventions.

'Well, I'm not going into the shop

with you carrying that!' said Sam.

'Nobody asked you,' said Posy sweetly, and watched him run off.

It was just her luck that Miss Perlethorpe should be in the Post Office, buying stamps. Posy and her bucket came creaking and clanking in and Miss Perlethorpe turned round.

'Oh Posy, it's you. Thank you, Mrs Parkins.'

'Miss Perlethorpe began sorting through her letters and sticking her stamps.

'Now Posy, what is it you wanted?'

Silently Posy handed over her list. One by one Mrs Parkins fetched and weighed out the items. Posy prayed that Miss Perlethorpe would go before she had to pay and put the things in her bucket. Something told her that Miss Perlethorpe would not see the point of going shopping with a coal-bucket.

But Miss Perlethorpe did not go. She stuck on the stamps with a maddening slowness, and then began looking at the various leaflets on the Post Office counter.

'There we are, then!' said Mrs

Parkins. 'Got your basket, dear?'

She went to the till, and Posy snatched up the things from the counter and dropped them into the bucket.

'Thank you!' She grabbed the change and made for the door, bucket clanking.

'Posy!'

She froze.

'Whatever . . . ? A *bucket*?'

'Here we go again!' thought Posy wearily.

She turned and faced Miss Perlethorpe.

The conversation she then had was almost exactly the same as the one she had just had with Sam. Except that now there was Mrs Parkins too, with her 'Well I nevers!' and 'Would you believes!'

At the end, Miss Perlethorpe said, 'If you are going to be an inventor, Posy, there are several things I would like to suggest. I wish you would invent a way of keeping your exercise books tidy, and getting to school on time. I also wish you would invent something to

59

keep your hair tidy and your shoes clean. And it is to be hoped that coal-dust does not get into your mother's bacon.'

Posy stamped home, clanking and glowering.

She went to see if Fred was awake. The good thing about him was that genius or not, he never answered back or criticized. Even when he bawled it

was nothing personal.

He lay cocooned in his pram under the wide green shelter of the orchard.

'Going to be an inventor, Fred,' she told him.

He gazed up with calm blue eyes.

'You know—invent new things.'

He did not seem excited. The trouble was, Posy thought, that being a baby, most things were new to him anyway.

'There are millions of things he hasn't seen yet,' she thought. 'Not even on the telly.'

This was an amazing thought.

'Don't worry, Fred,' she told him. 'I'll make sure you're clued up. I bet you're already the most clued-up baby in Little Paxton—in England, for all I know, England, Europe, the world, the universe!'

At this point Fred, disappointingly, shut his eyes.

'Oh well,' said Posy.

She did not wish to have the bucket conversation with Daff, so put the shopping into a plastic bag and left it on the draining-board, then went up to her hidey hole to think.

61

Being an inventor was not as easy as Posy had thought. She could think of things she'd like to invent, all right, but didn't know how to make them. She sat on her nest in the cupboard and made a list of the ten things she would most like to invent:

1. A brainwashing machine to make Mum let me have a dog.
2. A brainwashing machine to stop Mum picking on me.
3. A brainwashing machine to make Pearly forget to go to school every day.
4. A special whistle to make birds come and feed out of your hand.
5. A calendar with no Sundays.
6. An everlasting ice-cream.
7. An everlasting gob-stopper.
8. A calendar with Christmas every month.
9. A special dye to make my hair exactly the same colour as Emma Hawksworth's.
10. A dream machine.

She stared at the list long and hard and chewed on her pencil. It seemed very clear that none of these items could be made out of yoghurt pots.

'Don't know how to make *any* of them,' she admitted to Punch and Judy. 'Perhaps what I need to be is a witch, not an inventor.'

She picked up the magic bobbin that the bag lady had given her. She shook her head. She believed in it, all right, but it honestly did not look equal to getting rid of Sundays, or conjuring an everlasting ice-cream out of thin air.

She sighed deeply. She did not, however, give up. She decided to try a different approach.

'What I'll do is not invent new things,' she thought. 'I'll leave that till I'm grown up. What I'll do is invent new ways to use things that have already been invented. Like using the coal-bucket as a shopping basket. Now ... what shall I start with?'

She looked thoughtfully at Punch and Judy and Peg the Leg, but could not think of a single use for them.

'Except to put in Pearly's desk and frighten the life out of her,' she thought. 'Trouble is, it'd frighten the life out of *them*, as well. Cruelty to spiders and stick insects, that'd be.'

So she climbed out of the cupboard and looked round her room. What should she choose? Everything looked exceedingly boring and everyday, and to be used for one purpose and one purpose only. Still Posy did not give up.

'What I'll do, I'll shut my eyes and spin round. Then I'll open them, and the first thing I see, I'll invent a new way to use it. Even if it takes me all day to think of something.'

So she closed her eyes and spun and opened her eyes again and the first thing she saw was a sock.

'Oh, *gubbins*!' said Posy Bates.

She sat on the bed and looked coldly at the sock, which was pink-and-white striped and looked exactly what it was—a sock.

'That,' she said, 'is just my luck.'

But she had set herself a test.

'You couldn't wear it on your head as a hat,' she thought, 'not unless your head shrunk.'

The minutes ticked by on her Mickey Mouse clock.

'You couldn't use it as a pencil case.

64

It hasn't got a zip.'

Tick tock tick tock.

'You couldn't blow it up, like a balloon.'

Posy was making a very respectable list of things for which the sock couldn't be used. She supposed that made her the opposite of an inventor, whatever that was.

'A sock,' she thought glumly, 'is a sock. Full stop.'

Under her window she heard Fred begin to bawl.

'He's all bawl and bottle!' Posy said disgustedly, and was so pleased with the sound of it that she said it again, 'Bawl and bottle!'

And then she had the inspiration.

'Yippee!'

She snatched up the sock and ran out of her room and down the stairs. Daff was changing Fred's nappy. On the table stood his bottle, ready for the feed.

Posy picked it up and pulled on the sock. Perfect—it fitted like a glove—or a sock. It was, quite clearly, a bottle-sockle.

'There!'

Daff turned.

'Whatever?'

'Bottle-sockle!' Posy told her, triumphant. 'New invention! You know, like a tea-cosy or an egg-cosy. You're always saying the milk gets cold before he's finished.'

'But where's it *been*?' cried Daff. 'You were *wearing* that yesterday!'

Reluctantly Posy peeled the sock off the bottle. It did look rather grimy, now she looked at it.

'All right,' she said. 'But it is a good idea. It'd be perfect.'

'As a matter of fact,' said Daff slowly, 'it is a good idea. A very good idea. You run up and fetch a clean sock, Posy, and we'll use that.'

Posy raced back up to her room and rummaged for a clean sock.

'I did it!' she told her pets. 'I invented!'

And after that Fred's bottle always had a bottle-sockle. And after that it didn't matter when odd socks went missing. Instead of grumbling, as she always had, Daff would toss the odd

one into Fred's basket, saying,

'Here we are—another bottle-cosy!'

'Sockle!' Posy would tell her. 'Bottle-sockle!'

But it did not really matter. Sockle or cosy—what was the difference? Posy Bates was an inventor.

POSY BATES AT THE FAIR

It was Thursday—a good orange day, most of the week gone and Saturday in sight.

'Fun-fair tomorrow!' Posy told her pets. 'Ace! Total!'

Neither spiders nor stick insect stirred a feeler.

'Wakes, Mum and Dad say. "Little Paxton Wakes". That's what they've called it, ever since they were little. Ages ago—can't even *imagine* them little, specially Mum. She says she had pigtails! Says the boys used to pull 'em till her whole head hurt. Wakes! Says she used to save her sixpences for months before. No such thing as sixpences now, of course. That was what she got for pocket-money. Says sixpences were small and silver and a bit like 20p's, except that they were round, not with bitten-off edges. Not that you know about money, of course. The thing is, *I've* been saving, for ages. And I'm going to go on rides and things, but the main reason is I'm going to win a goldfish or bust!'

This was a very long speech. It was certainly much longer than she could have made to her family, for instance. Families have a habit of interrupting. The beauty of having Punch and Judy and Peg the Leg to talk to, was the way they just listened. And the fact that they could not utter a single word even if they tried, made them ideal for telling her secrets to. The matter of the goldfish was, of course, Top Secret.

A goldfish, while not needing to be taken for walks, and not having kittens every five minutes, certainly counted as a pet. Posy's mother was very firm on this point—No Pets. She did not even approve of spiders and stick insects,

which was why Posy had to keep them in her hidey-hole. She gazed at them now with affection.

'Don't suppose you know about goldfish,' she told them. 'Or any fish, come to that.'

She had found Punch and Judy in the shed and Peg the Leg in the raspberry canes. They came from very small worlds.

She decided to give them a lecture on the subject of fish.

'Fish aren't like you and me,' she explained. 'They don't live in air, they live in water. Don't know how they breathe, but they do. Not through noses, of course, because they haven't got noses.' She paused. 'Nor have you, come to that. Funny ... wonder what *you* breathe through ... I'm not criticizing, you look very nice without noses, in fact I can't imagine you with.'

At this point she shut her eyes and tried to imagine spiders and stick insects with noses, and failed.

'I just expect your noses are really tiny,' she told them. 'Don't worry—they suit you. Anyway, fish live in the sea and rivers and things, but goldfish are really posh. They really *are* gold—beautiful, shiny, orangey gold, and they live in bowls. At least, the ones that live in houses do. Some of them live in ponds under lily pads. I've seen them, in Mrs Cartwright's garden. Anyway, the point is this. I can't go and *buy* a goldfish, because Mum wouldn't let me, and if I did she'd make me take it back. But if I *win* one, that's different. If you win something, that's that. It shows you're meant to have it.'

The logic of this seemed perfect and unarguable.

'I've already got some goldfish food. I shall keep it up here and it'll be company for you. I might even teach it some tricks.'

She paused again while she pondered this. She could not, she thought, teach a goldfish to sit and stay, or fetch sticks. Or sit up and beg. And she had not had much luck teaching tricks to Punch and Judy or Peg the Leg. But she would think of something, she had no doubt.

'Anyway, I'll keep it up here,' she continued, 'and if you watch it sailing round and round I dare say it'll help you to get to sleep.'

She was on safer ground here. She sometimes went to visit old Mrs Kettleborough, who was ninety-three and had a proper aquarium with seven fish for company.

'I talk to them regular,' she told Posy, 'and they understand every word I say. And when I have my afternoon nap, I'll just sit here and look at them going round and round and round, and I'll feel myself going dreamy like, then I'm fast asleep in two ticks.'

Posy now wondered if it was quite tactful to sing the praises of goldfish quite so much to her other pets.

'There's no need to be jealous,' she told them. 'I shan't like it any better than you. Mum says that even if you have ten children you still love them all just as much. Though I don't know how she knows.'

She sat thoughtfully for a moment, then scrambled out of the cupboard. She counted the money in her pot pig

72

for the umpteenth time. Satisfied that there was enough and to spare to win a goldfish, she went down and into the garden.

There she practised rolling table tennis balls, which was what you had to do to win a goldfish. She had made lanes on a wide piece of chipboard, using strips of a broken seed-box. She then tilted the wood by resting it on a stone. She had already spent hours rolling ping-pong balls down it, and was sure she now had the hang of it.

As she practised she heard the heavy rumble of wheels. She looked up to see a painted yellow van go past the gate. It did not have Fun-Fair written on the side, but it might just as well have done. Later, she would go up to the green with Sam and watch the rides and stalls being put up.

She went over to the budding genius in the pram to fill him in about fun-fairs and goldfish. She picked him up and twizzled him round to demonstrate roundabouts, and he seemed to like it.

'Could even take you down the helter-skelter, I s'pose,' she told him. 'I could hold you on my lap. But I shouldn't think Mum'd let me.'

(She was right. Daff was horrified by the suggestion.)

'But the best thing,' Posy told Fred as she lowered him back into his pram, still gurgling, 'is that I'm going to win a goldfish. And to be sure I *do* win, I'm going to do my magic spell before I go. You know—I told you about it. Twice round the garden shed, once round the sundial, clap your hands five times, shut your eyes and say the magic word. Which is *so* magic, Fred Bates, that I'm not saying it, not even to you!'

The fair opened at noon the next day. Posy tipped the contents of her pig into her purse. She then went and performed her magic ritual which she had invented years ago, and found a great comfort. She went twice round the garden shed, once round the sundial, clapped her hands five times, shut her eyes and said the magic word. She let out a deep breath, opened her eyes and felt that the goldfish was as good as hers.

Then she called for Sam and they set

off for the green, with Pippa in charge.

'Fun-fair!' Pippa scoffed. 'Just a few baby roundabouts. Not a real fair at all.'

She meant not like the Goose Fair in Nottingham. That was, Posy admitted, amazing. For three days in October it sprawled like a giant fun city over the wide slopes of the Forest. At night the blazing lights could be seen, and the excited hum heard, for miles around.

Nonetheless, Posy thought, Little Paxton Wakes were not to be sneezed at, and the goldfish were as dazzling and desirable as any the Goose Fair had to offer. She could hear music and screams, and saw the striped finger of the helter-skelter. The village green was transformed, made magical.

Posy was so excited that she raced ahead with Sam, and was soon swinging as high as the trees and level with roof-tops. Next she rode round and round and up and down on a dappled grey horse. The world went into a bright blur. She raced and screamed her steep way down the helter-skelter.

'Must save some money for the goldfish,' she reminded herself at the top. By the time she rolled off her mat at the bottom, she had forgotten.

Now she was dizzy and the world was definitely not standing still. She staggered off to sit for a minute on the grass verge and that was when she saw the bag lady. *Her* bag lady.

You could have knocked her over with a feather. The ramshackle old lady of the Victoria Centre was hunched on the bench under the giant chestnut for all the world as if she had taken root there.

Posy went over on her wobbling legs. 'Hello!'

The bag lady looked at her. She did not smile—it was hard to imagine her ever smiling—but Posy knew that she was recognized.

'Fancy seeing you! I can't believe it!'

She couldn't, either. Peaceful, ordinary Little Paxton seemed a strange setting for so rare and exotic a bird.

'I live here,' Posy told her. 'Down that way.' She pointed. 'Last house on the left.'

She wondered immediately whether it was tactful to mention houses to one who slept in cardboard boxes under bridges.

'It's quite boring, actually, living here,' she said. 'Not interesting, like you. Travelling round, I mean.'

When it came to conversation, the bag lady was not much better than Punch and Judy or Peg the Leg.

'Have you been on any rides?'

Another silly remark. Would the bag

lady really lug her bulging bags to the top of the helter-skelter, or pile them into a dodgem car? On the other hand, Posy thought, she might *like* a ride, if it weren't for the bags.

'If you want to go on something, I'll keep an eye on your bags,' she offered.

The bag lady did give a kind of snort at that, which was better than nothing. And now she was really looking at Posy, eyes bright under bristling eyebrows.

'Can't ride on an empty belly,' she said.

'Of course not!'

Posy had forgotten that underneath the roly-poly cocoon of garments the bag lady was thin and hungry with a rumbling belly.

'Hang on!' she said, and made for the hot dog stand. She ordered two 'with onions, please'.

She took them back to the bench and the two of them sat rudely and noisily champing their hot dogs, just as they had sat in the Victoria Centre.

'I might be able to show you my sister,' Posy said through a mouthful, 'she's here somewhere. Fred's at home, though. Only a baby.'

The bag lady made no reply. She did not even seem to be listening. Posy did not care. She was ten times more interesting silent than most people were talking. Not that she was exactly silent. She champed and swallowed and gulped and her teeth clattered. Her nose snorted and snuffled. Posy wished that Pippa would come, or Sam, and see her sitting side by side and thick as thieves with a real live bag lady. She rather hoped, however, that her mother would not.

'Now for afters!' she said.

She stood in a queue at the ice-cream van and bought two double cones with chocolate flakes.

The bag lady snatched hers without a word. Posy was not in the least offended. She was positive that the old lady was truly grateful, whether she said 'thank you' or not. 'Thank you' didn't necessarily mean anything. You could say 'thank you' without even meaning it. Posy had done so herself thousands of times.

'I expect it's a bit of a treat for you, being at a fair,' said Posy. 'Even if you don't go on anything.'

The bag lady was licking her chops. A blob of ice-cream hung on her chin. '*I* know what! We've had afters—now we'll have *after* afters!'

What she meant was candy-floss, great soft sticky pink clouds of it. Candy-floss was much more of a treat than hot dogs and ice-cream. You could only get it at fairs, or at the seaside.

'Though I don't see why,' she thought. 'I don't expect there's a *law* about it.'

The bag lady eyed the candy-floss warily. She took it, but did not seem to know how to tackle it. Posy understood her difficulty. You couldn't wolf candy-floss, even if you tried. You had to go at it softly, to nuzzle and tease it with your tongue. It looked so puffed up and enormous that it was always surprising how tiny it felt in your mouth. It was almost like eating thin air. Sweet thin air.

A lot of the bag lady's floss ended up on her mitts and coat and even in her hair. She looked like an overgrown toddler, as if a mother should swoop down on her and clean her up.

'Hasn't got a mother though, I don't expect,' Posy thought. 'Or brothers or sisters or anything. Not even a pet.'

That was when she remembered the goldfish. She felt for her purse, so fat and heavy when she had set out, and now gone thin and light.

'Enough there for one or two goes,' she thought. 'You never know your luck.'

She stood up.

'I'm just going to one of the stalls to win something,' she said. 'I'll bring it back to show you.'

The bag lady said nothing, not even 'Good luck!'

Posy knew that she would be very lucky indeed to win a goldfish in only two goes. She had meant to leave enough money for twenty goes, at least.

She gazed at the shining goldfish, handed over her money and started to roll. But the slant of the board was different, or else the ping-pong balls were. They seemed to go their own way, not the way she rolled them, or willed them to roll. The last ball went down. Nothing.

Posy looked again at the goldfish. She dug deep in her pocket, hoping to find an odd coin. Her heart jumped. There was one—and something else as well. She drew out her hand and stared down at a ten pence piece—and the bag lady's lucky bobbin.

It was a sign, Posy knew it.

'Third time lucky,' she thought.

'*And* a lucky bobbin. Here we go!'

And the balls rolled smoothly and obediently into their slots, and next minute she was holding a bag of clear water with a bright, flickering goldfish.

She had dreamed of how it would feel to have the prize in her hand. Now that it had happened, she could hardly believe it. She turned and walked slowly away, not taking her eyes off it, feeling that everyone else's eyes were on her with her prize.

It was the magic bobbin that had done it. She knew it in her bones. The bobbin given her by a bag lady who had no mother and father, no brothers and sisters, not even a pet. The bag lady wandered the world alone, a world that was wide and draughty.

Posy Bates knew what she must do, so she did not even stop to think about it. She marched straight to the bench under the chestnut and laid her silvery-gold treasure on the bag lady's lap.

'Here you are,' she said. 'A pet. To keep you company.'

She even managed to smile before

turning and running for home, pockets empty and eyes stinging. She ran past Daff and Fred and up to her room and into the dim comfort of the cupboard.

'I don't care,' she told the three of them. 'Silly things, anyway, goldfish are. No noses and no legs.'

She sniffed for a while, and then cheered up at the thought of the bag lady going to sleep that night in a cardboard box under a bridge with a goldfish for company.

When she went back down, Pippa was home too.

'What did you run off like that for?' she demanded. 'You're supposed to tell me—isn't she, Mum?'

'She certainly is,' said Daff. 'Do you never stop to think, Posy Bates? Your sister was looking for you everywhere.'

'Sorry,' said Posy.

She wandered out into the garden. Over the fence she saw Sam with a pail of water. He looked up and saw her.

'Hey—come and look what I've got!'

Posy went. She stared glumly down at the fish, which was not shimmering gold as hers had been, merely orange.

'How many goes did it take to win?'

'None!' He was triumphant. 'It was fantastic. There was this mucky old woman on a bench, and she gave it to me!'

Posy stared.

'She just said, "Here—you take it!", and shoved it at me, and that was that!'

Posy looked again at the fish and saw that it was golden, after all. She said nothing.

That night she cried again into her pillow. She did not know whether she was crying for her lost goldfish or for the bag lady, still wandering the wide, draughty world alone. And all night long her dreams were woven of hooting trains and hollow bridges where silvery goldfish swooped and flew like a shoal of birds.

POSY BATES GOES GREEN

'You're not supposed to do that,' said Posy Bates, watching her mother spray her newly-set hair.

'Oh no?' You could tell Daff was not really listening.

'No. It goes up in the sky and makes holes in it.'

'What? These few puffs?'

'Not just those few puffs. Everybody's few puffs and squirts. They all add up together and make this big hole.'

'Well, I have heard that,' admitted Daff. 'But I don't use a lot.'

'And fly spray,' Posy went on, 'and polish spray and that horrible air-freshener. Pooh—what a stink! That smells nothing *like* fresh air.'

'You've got to kill wasps and polish furniture,' Daff said.

'Ah, but you can get special squirters,' Posy told her. 'Pearly says so.'

'I'm surprised you ever listen to a

word Miss Perlethorpe says,' said Daff.

'I don't much,' Posy said. 'If there's one thing I'm never going to be when I grow up, it's a teacher like her.'

'What are you going to be, then?' It was Pippa, come to borrow Daff's hair spray.

'An expert,' said Posy promptly. She did not know why she said it. The words just came, as if they had been waiting to be said.

'An expert on what?'

'Nothing. Just an expert.'

'You can't be just an expert can you, Mum?' said Pippa. 'You have to be an expert *on* something.'

Posy cast wildly about.

'Birds and beasts,' she said. Those words came out of the blue, too. 'Birds and beasts and especially insects.'

'Oh—creepy-crawlies!' Pippa was scornful. 'You've got spiders on the brain, Posy Bates!'

'Insects are important,' Posy told her. 'It says so, in my book. We need them.'

'Well, I don't, that I am sure of,' said Daff.

'Anyway, spiders are better than hair sprays, that I *do* know!' and Posy marched out of the room.

Little did they know that up in Posy's big cupboard there were three caterpillars in a jam-jar waiting to turn into something. She was not sure what.

'Whatever they are, they'll be company for you,' she had told Punch and Judy and Peg the Leg.

At least one of them might be a dragon, she rather hoped. She knew that there was not much chance of this, but there was no harm in wishing. If a dragon did emerge, she very much hoped it would breathe fire. This would scare the pants off Miss Perlethorpe and might be useful for cooking. She did not think this fire would be polluting.

Oddly enough, the very next day Miss Perlethorpe announced to the school that there was to be a special event at the end of term.

'A special Green Event,' she told them. 'We shall plant three trees on the village green, for posterity.'

The children themselves were to raise the money to buy the trees.

'You can run errands and do odd jobs,' she said. 'Or perhaps hold little Bring and Buys. Many a mickle makes a muckle.'

'Whatever *that* means!' said Sam Post under his breath.

Posy thought she knew what it meant, and she liked the sound of it.

'Many a mickle makes a muckle,' she chanted under her breath on the way home. 'Many a pickle makes a puckle. Many a tickle makes a tuckle...'

'I shall wash cars to make my money,' Sam told her. 'What'll you do?'

'Dunno. Haven't decided yet.'

Posy went up into her cupbaord after tea, to think about it.

'Not something boring,' she told Punch and Judy and Peg the Leg. 'Not like running errands or washing cars. Something special.'

They did not, of course, reply. And it seemed to Posy (even though she could not exactly see their eyes) that they gazed dolefully back at her. It occurred to her that their own lives must be very boring up here in the cupboard, and she felt a pang of guilt.

'I'd better let them out,' she thought. 'I'd better not collect any more.'

The thought was unbearably sad. She was used to their company. She would miss them. They blurred and swam as her eyes filled. Then came the inspiration.

'A Pet Show!'

That was it. She would hold a Pet Show in the garden and charge to come in.

'And you'll be in it!' she told them. 'You'll be the most unusual pets there! The rest will be boring old cats and dogs and hamsters. You'll be the stars!'

The spiders and the stick insect showed few signs of excitement, but Posy was sure they had understood.

She spent the rest of the evening making two posters, on the backs of empty cornflakes packets.

'GREAT GREEN PET SHOW. 11 O'clock Saturday morning at 27 Green Lane. Bring your pets. PRIZES for best pet judged by POSY BATES, EXPERT in Birds and Beasts especially Insects. Entrance 20p ADULTS, 10p CHILDREN.'

She added a picture of a ginger cat with whiskers of an unlikely length, and was satisfied. Next morning she

took the posters down to breakfast.

'Never thought of asking me first, I suppose?' said Daff when she saw them.

'I can, can't I, Mum?' Posy begged.

'Oh, go on then,' Daff told her.

'Bird and beast expert!' scoffed Pippa.

'But no snakes, mind,' warned Daff. 'I do draw the line there.'

'People in Little Paxton don't *have* snakes, Mum,' Pippa told her.

'You never know,' said Daff. 'You can't tell by people's faces whether they've got snakes.'

This, Posy thought, was true. And her mother certainly was scared of snakes. She would scream even if she caught sight of one on television. To be on the safe side, Posy added 'No snakes by request', then pinned one poster on the front gate and took the other to school.

'Very nice, Posy,' Miss Perlethorpe told her. 'It is most original and extremely Green. You may pin it on the wall next to the Window Monitor list.'

That evening Posy found some blue

ribbon and spent a happy time making it into a rosette. In the middle she stuck a white disc saying '1st Prize'.

She looked dubiously at Punch and Judy.

'Ought to be two really, I suppose,' she told them. 'But the thing is, I can't pin it on you anyway. So what I'll do, I'll just stick it on your jam-jar.'

The spiders were asleep, or pretending to be.

'I think perhaps I'll give it to you, instead,' she told Peg the Leg. 'Yes, that's better. If I give it to two, the others might say it was cheating.'

Next day she asked Sam Post to help her.

'You can collect the money,' she said.

'I'm bringing my goldfish,' he told her. 'Bet he'll win.'

It was lucky he did not know the judge had already made up her mind. Even if a llama or giraffe turned up at Posy Bates' Pet Show, first prize would still go to a stick insect.

On Saturday morning the pets started arriving at about ten o'clock. First came Carol Boot, carrying a wicker basket from which came a lot of mewing and squeaking.

'It's Priscilla,' she announced, 'and her three kittens. They're called Smudge, Bing and Topsy, and they're bound to win first prize.'

'You'll have to open the basket for the judging,' Posy told her. 'I can't see them.'

Not that it would make any

difference if she could.

Then came Billy Martin, towing his huge Old English sheep-dog, Ben.

'He's got a pedigree a mile long,' he said. 'My ma said he could go to Cruft's, if we wanted. He'll win first prize, all right.'

He looked scornfully at the dog Mary Pye was leading in.

'We got him from the RSPCA,' she told Posy. 'His name's Buster. I've trained him to find bits of chocolate and open and shut doors. He bit the postman last week, but it was a mistake. My dad says he's gentle as a lamb.'

Buster bared his teeth and growled softly. Posy dropped back a few paces.

'Well, don't let him off his lead,' she said. 'All dogs to be kept on leads. Ooo—look!'

Vicky Wright came trotting round the house on her donkey, Patch.

'Can I have a ride?' begged Posy.

'All right.' Vicky climbed down and Posy got on. It was amazing how high up she felt. The world looked quite different.

'Gee up!' she cried. The donkey did not budge.

'Gee up!'

'He only goes when he feels like it,' Vicky told her. 'You'll have to wait.'

Posy, disappointed, waited. From her vantage point she watched a procession of pets arriving. There were more cats in baskets and cardboard boxes—at least, she supposed they were cats. She certainly hoped they were not snakes. There were mice, hamsters, a tortoise and a whole assortment of dogs.

Miss Perlethorpe was among the last to arrive, leading her white poodle, Selina. She looked about her at the motley assortment of pets and owners.

'Oh, there you are, Posy. Who is organizing? Where is your mother?'

'Inside,' Posy told her. 'It's my Pet Show. I'm organizing.'

'You cannot do that from the back of a donkey,' Miss Perlethorpe told her. '*I* had better organize.'

She clapped her hands. No one noticed, let alone paid any attention.

Posy saw that Ben Briggs' billy-goat had arrived, and was chewing one of the cat baskets—the owner seemed to have disappeared.

'It's a good selection,' she thought happily. 'Cats, dogs, tortoises, hamsters, mice, goldfish, spiders, stick insects, budgies, donkeys, goats...'

She felt that her Pet Show was already a huge success.

'Girls! Boys!' cried Miss Perlethorpe in ringing tones. 'Billy—come down from that tree! Come here, everyone, at once!'

Reluctantly her pupils abandoned their games, and gathered round sulkily. They did not expect to be bossed on a Saturday as well as on weekdays.

'Now I want you to form an orderly circle,' she told them. 'Each stand by your pet, ready for the judging.'

They shuffled into an untidy ring. The dogs were now panting and straining at their leashes.

'You are surely not going to judge from the back of a donkey?' Miss Perlethorpe asked Posy. 'You must inspect each animal carefully. You cannot do that from up there.'

'I can,' replied Posy. She did not mention that she had already decided that the blue rosette would go to Peg the Leg. 'I can see them all really clearly.'

'But what about the cats?' Miss Perlethorpe persisted. 'You must come down and look in the baskets.'

'Yes, it's not fair!' yelled the cat owners.

'My decision is final,' announced Posy. She knew that this was a good remark for a judge to make. 'Open the baskets!'

The baskets were opened. So too, it seemed, was Pandora's box. The moment the lids went up, out sprang cats and kittens like jack-in-the-boxes. The dogs jerked their leads from their owners' grasps and were after them in a flash. The billy-goat followed suit and he chased the dogs while the dogs chased the cats. The children, shrieking, chased anything that moved.

Patch the donkey picked that moment to move. Posy had not known a donkey could move so fast.

'Help!' she screamed, as Patch careered through the garden, kicking mouse-cages and boxes left and right.

'Posy, you come back here this minute!' she heard her mother screech.

'Chance'd be a fine thing!' Posy thought.

She could do nothing at all with the donkey, tug and yell 'Stop!' as she

99

might. In the end she gave up and concentrated on not falling off.

She glimpsed dogs, cats, goats in a whirligig, and her scampering friends and the horrified face of Miss Perlethorpe. She felt very unlike an Expert in Birds, Beasts Especially Insects. It seemed like hours she clung on for grim life, and when the end of the ride came, she saw it coming.

'No! Oh no!' she screamed, as the donkey headed straight for the little orchard with its low-hanging boughs.

'Here we go!' she remembered thinking, and then the donkey ran straight under an apple tree and Posy was scraped off his back and bump, down on to the tussocky grass.

'Am I alive?' wondered Posy Bates. Then, 'Couldn't be wondering if I *was* alive if I wasn't alive, so I must be!'

'You great lunatic!' It was Pippa, panting above her. 'You all right?'

'I—think so,' Posy said.

'Oooh, you goof! Come on!' Pippa was tugging Posy to her feet, then hugging her. 'Honestly, Posy!'

Posy did not get hugged a lot by Pippa.

'She really likes me,' she thought happily. 'She's glad I'm not dead!'

Daff was next on the scene. For a moment Pippa and she were practically fighting over Posy.

'Oh, thank heaven! Are you sure you haven't got concussion? That donkey ought not to be loose!'

Patch was now aimlessly meandering through the orchard as if butter would not melt in his mouth. In the distance

Posy could hear her friends still screaming and dogs barking and, above the pandemonium, the voice of Miss Perlethorpe.

'Go home! Do you hear me? This minute! Every one of you collect your pets and *go home!*'

'Old bossy-boots!' murmured Posy, her face pressed into Daff's cardigan.

'Yes, you take that donkey, Vicky Wright!' she heard Daff say. 'And don't bring it here again!'

'Posy could've been dead!' Pippa yelled for good measure. 'Wasn't *her* fault she fell off!'

Posy was really rather enjoying all this. Fred was the only one in the family who usually came in for this sort of attention.

In the distance the screams and barking faded, then died away.

'Come on then, love,' said Daff. 'Are you all right to walk?'

'Dunno,' said Posy. Her legs did feel rather wonky.

'You hold on to me,' Daff told her.

The trio went slowly back towards the house. Posy's Green Pet Show had disappeared altogether—even Sam Post and his goldfish. Miss Perlethorpe had made a good job of clearing everyone off. There was not a sign of life, except . . .

Posy caught her breath. There, sitting right in the middle of the patch of grass, and facing her, as if he were waiting for her, was one lone dog. She knew for a fact that he had not been brought to the Pet Show, for the simple reason that she had not noticed him. And this dog, above all others, she would have noticed, because he was, exactly, the dog of her dreams.

His fur was long and black, mostly, though she could see a patch of white here and there. It was so long that she could hardly see his eyes. He stood up. It *was* the dog of her dreams! There were the shaggy legs ending in great furry paws, round and big as saucers.

'Look!' said Pippa. 'There's one left. Come on, boy!'

The dog was wagging his tail now, a great waving plume. He advanced, but he was coming not to Pippa, but straight to Posy herself.

'Good boy!' she heard her voice croak. Then she could see his eyes, brown and pleading, and she fell to her knees and buried her face and arms in his soft coat.

'Posy! Are you all right? Oh dear, it is concussion!'

Posy heard her mother's voice as if it were a long way off or in another dimension. She did not exactly *think* 'Now, now's the moment if ever I'm to get a dog! This is it! She's so glad I'm not dead she'll give me anything. Now!'

She did not think this, but some instinct told her that it was true, though she hardly dared believe it. After years of spiders and stick insects in jars, of hedgehogs and chrysalides, was this warm, furry, solid creature really to be hers? A voice in another layer of her mind was jabbering, 'Twice round the garden shed, once round the sundial, clap your hands five times, shut your eyes and say the magic word!' She put a hand in her pocket for the comforting feel of the bag lady's magic bobbin. She mustered all the magic at her command.

When she did finally raise her face it was wet with tears.

'Oh Posy, love,' Daff said, 'what is it?'

Posy Bates shook her head. For once in her life words would not come. She heard Daff heave a long sigh.

'I can see what's coming,' she said. 'Come along, then. Better keep it, I suppose, till someone claims it.'

And the tears in Posy's eyes were all

at once rainbows because the sun, it seemed, had come out for ever. But that is another story . . .

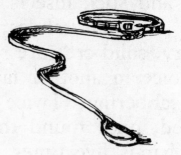

Photoset, printed and bound in Great Britain by REDWOOD PRESS LIMITED, Melksham, Wiltshire